Hey Hippopotamus Do Babies Eat Cake Too?

Hey HIPPOPOTAMUS Do Babies Eat Cake Too?

by Hazel Edwards

illustrated by Deborah Niland

PUFFIN BOOKS

For the Hogan family

PUFFIN BOOKS

UK | USA | Canada | Ireland | Australia
India | New Zealand | South Africa | China

Penguin Books is part of the Penguin Random House group of companies whose addresses can be found at global.penguinrandomhouse.com.

First published by Hodder Headline Australia Pty Ltd 1992
This edition published by Penguin Random House Australia Pty Ltd 2018

Offset from the Hodder Headline edition
Cover design by Karen Scott © Penguin Random House Australia Pty Ltd
Colour separation by Splitting Image Colour Studio, Clayton, Victoria
Printed and bound in China

A catalogue record for this book is available from the National Library of Australia

ISBN: 978 0 14 350139 8 (paperback)

Penguin Random House Australia uses papers that are natural and recyclable products, made from wood grown in sustainable forests. The logging and manufacture processes are expected to conform to the environmental regulations of the country of origin

penguin.com.au

Mummy is having a baby.
She told me.
'When?' I ask.
'Soon,' she says. 'The baby will belong to all of us.'

I've got a daddy and a big brother, but we haven't had a baby before.
So I told my hippopotamus who lives on the roof and eats cake.
He knows everything about babies.

Then I ask Mummy, 'Is our baby in your tummy now?'
She nods.
Was I in your tummy too?'
'Yes.'
'Why didn't I see the baby then?'
Mummy and Daddy laugh.
But my hippopotamus knows what I mean.

My brother and I play football.
'Will the baby be able to play football?' I ask.
'Not for a while,' Daddy says.
My hippopotamus on the roof can play anything.

'What's the baby's name?'
Mummy smiles. 'We haven't chosen a name yet.'
That's all right.
My hippopotamus doesn't have a name.
But he's always there on the roof, eating cake.

Our baby has a room
and a cot
and a bath
and millions of nappies.
But the baby has no name.
We haven't chosen it yet.
My hippopotamus is thinking of a name.

Grandma is in the kitchen.
We make pizza.
She asks me, 'Is the baby's name PIZZA?'
We laugh.
I say, 'No!'

Aunty fixes my bike in the garage.
We make a mess.
She asks me, 'Is the baby's name BIKE?'
We laugh.
I say, 'No!'

Daddy paints the bedroom.
Paint falls on me.
I ask, 'What colour will the baby be?'
'Wait and see,' Daddy says.
My hippopotamus on the roof knows all *his* colours.

Daddy washes my hair.
It is wet and shiny.
I ask, 'Will the baby have hair?'
'Wait and see,' Daddy says.
My hippopotamus hasn't got any hair but he's got a lovely wig.

Grandpa reads me a story.
He takes off his glasses.
His eyes are brown.
I ask, 'What colour will our baby's eyes be?'
'Wait and see.'
My hippopotamus can see everything from up on the roof.

The man at the shop asks, ‘Do you want a brother or a sister?’

I don’t know.

Sometimes I’d like to have a baby.

Other times I don’t want one.

My hippopotamus wants the baby to look like me.

Uncle gives me a dolly in a cot.
'What's your dolly's name?' he asks.
I don't know yet.
Uncle smiles. 'Is it a No-Name Dolly?'
I say, 'Yes.'
My hippopotamus knows *my* name because it's on my clothes.
And he *has* got a name, really, but it's our secret.

Early this morning, Daddy woke me up.
'Our baby's here,' he said.
I went to see the No-Name Baby.
It was red, squashy and beautiful.
Daddy told me the baby's name.
And it's just right.

Baby drinks only milk.
But my hippop tamus saved some cake for later.
He knows everything about babies.